The Pocket Dog

The Pocket Dog

HOLLY WEBB

Illustrated by Sharon Rentta

■ SCHOLASTIC

First published in the UK in 2016 by Scholastic Children's Books
An imprint of Scholastic Ltd
Euston House, 24 Eversholt Street, London, NW1 1DB, UK
Registered office: Westfield Road, Southam, Warwickshire, CV47 0RA
SCHOLASTIC and associated logos are trademarks and/or
registered trademarks of Scholastic Inc.

ISBN 978 1407 14488 7

A CIP catalogue record for this book
is available from the British Library.

Printed by CPI Group (UK) Ltd, Croydon, CR0 4YY
Papers used by Scholastic Children's Books are made
from wood grown in sustainable forests.

1 3 5 7 9 10 8 6 4 2

www.scholastic.co.uk
www.hollywebb.om

For dachshund fans everywhere!

1

"Look at him!" Kitty leaned over, wrapping her arms around her tummy. She'd already laughed so much that her ribs ached, and she just couldn't stop. "Oh, look at his ears!"

"She's gone." Kitty's younger brother Luke rolled his eyes at his twin, Sam. "You sound like a hyena, Kitty."

"A really crazy hyena," Sam agreed. "What's so funny, anyway? He's just running."

"But his ears!" Kitty wailed. "And the bouncing."

Luke snorted, but he was grinning too.

"Watch it," Sam put in. "If you don't stop

laughing like that you'll be sick."

Kitty gasped in a whooping breath and tried very hard to stop giggling. She had a feeling Sam might be right, even though obviously she'd never tell him. The thing was, every time she stopped laughing, Frank would start racing around in the long grass again. He was a very, very small dachshund, and he couldn't see over the top of the grass, so he had to bounce to see where he was going. He bounced across the field towards them now, his huge golden ears flapping madly.

"Frankie! Frankie, come here." Luke patted his knees, and the little dachshund flung himself at him, barking excitedly. He whirled around Luke's ankles, yapping and dancing, and Luke dabbed at him with the lead, trying to get it back on.

"Stand still, you dim dog." Sam crouched down to hold him still. "Oi! Don't lick me. Ugh, Frankie, you know I hate lick. Ow! Ow! Get him off me..." He stumbled backwards giggling, trying to escape Frank's pink tongue, but Frank was delighted that Sam was lower down than usual, and better for licking. He jumped at Sam, barking and licking and wagging all at the same

time, and Sam teetered over backwards into the grass.

Frank peered down at him with interest; and licked him again, since he was lying there in just the right place. Then he sat down on Sam's chest and started to scratch one ear with his hind paw. The grass seeds were in his fur, and they made him itchy.

Kitty's mum and dad arrived a few minutes later. They were walking with Shadow, who was slowing down now that he was twelve, so they'd been a way behind. When they came out from between the trees, Kitty was still making squeaky laugh noises and gasping so much that she'd had to sit down. Luke had just managed to get the lead out from underneath Sam and attach it to Frank's collar, and Sam was spreadeagled in the grass staring at the sky and moaning about dog spit, with the tiny creamy-golden dachshund sitting proudly on his chest.

"Hi, Mum. Hi, Dad," Kitty wheezed. "Hi, Shadow." The black Labrador gazed back at them all, and Kitty was sure he looked disapproving. Even before his stiff legs had slowed him down, he'd never behaved like this. He'd come from a breeder who trained all her puppies beautifully, and then he'd been to obedience classes and agility training. Several of his relatives were police dogs, and he was very dignified. He did not sit on people, or even on the sofa. Not even now, when he was elderly and aching and would have found a sofa very comfortable indeed, if only he could have got on to it. Instead he usually lay flopped over Dad's feet, looking adoring. He was a bit of a one-man dog.

Now he leaned down to touch noses with Frankie, and Frankie nuzzled him back. Then the little puppy sprang off Sam's chest to weave in and out of Shadow's paws and nibble his ankles.

Sam started to struggle up off the grass. "Oooof... Mum, did you bring wipes? Frankie kept licking me, I'm all sticky."

"No, I didn't. You look nice and clean, actually. I suppose you shouldn't let him lick you though, Sam, it's not really a good idea!"

"I didn't let him! He pushed me over!"

Kitty started to snort with laughter again, looking down at tiny, delicate Frankie, and then Sam, who was quite big for eight.

Mum sighed and shook her head. "You let that dog walk all over you— What? Kitty, don't laugh, I'm serious! You know the lady we got him from said that dachshunds can be very bossy if you don't show them you're in charge."

"It's just funny." Kitty took a deep, shaky breath and closed her eyes. Her tummy was actually properly hurting now from laughing so much. "Because he's so tiny, but he's so bossy. He's like the bossiest person I've ever met. And he *did* walk all over Sam. . ."

Her mum grinned. "I see what you mean. OK, it *is* quite funny. But we need to get back – I reckon it's going to pour down soon. Look at those clouds coming over."

Everyone looked round to peer over the top of the trees at the dark mass of clouds.

"They're nowhere close," Luke protested. "Can't we go on a bit further and get to the stream?"

"Nope." Dad shook his head. "Shadow needs time to do the walk back, and so does Frankie. Look at them."

Shadow had collapsed down on to the grass, easing his legs out in front of him and resting his greying muzzle on his paws. Frankie had flumped down on Shadow's paws too. His eyes were closed, and one of his long feathery ears was draped over Shadow's nose. Shadow looked as though he hated it, but he was just too polite to say so.

"And I bet you haven't finished your

homework," Mum reminded the boys. "Didn't you have a list of spellings to learn?"

"Uuurrgh." Sam heaved a huge sigh. "Weekends shouldn't be for homework."

"That'd be a yes then. Come on. Home time." Dad crouched down to stroke Shadow's head. "Let's go, Shadow. Good boy."

The old Labrador started to struggle up, but Frankie wouldn't get off his paws. He was completely floppy, like a toy dog, and as Shadow stood up, Frankie slid down into the grass. He didn't wake up properly, just snorted and wriggled himself into a ball.

Luke pulled gently on his lead, but Frankie only curled up tighter. He tucked his nose under his tail, and Kitty was sure she could hear tiny little puppy snores.

"Shall I carry him?" she suggested, reaching down to scoop her hands underneath the warm fur.

Dad smiled. "No, don't worry, I will. It's not fair, is it, Shadow? No one's going to carry you, are they? Give him here, Kitty." He tucked Frankie under his arm, but the dachshund was so little he just slipped around saggily as they walked along.

"I don't suppose you feel like waking up and walking?" Dad muttered as he stopped to hitch Frankie up again.

"I know!" Kitty pulled up the flap on the big side pocket of Dad's raincoat. "Put him in there."

Dad laughed. "He wouldn't stay."

"I bet he would, Dad; he's fast asleep. It's because he's got such little legs, it's like he's walked twice as far as everybody else. And he kept running after squirrels." She pulled the pocket open wider as Dad shuffled the sleepy dog inside. "Look! He's a perfect fit! Oh, Dad, he's a pocket dog!" She giggled as Frankie opened one dark eye to check what was going on. He slumped comfortably into the pocket, with just his muzzle and the edge of an eye poking out at the top. He looked quite happy.

Dad grinned. "Well, it's definitely easier that way. He'll probably want to be carried every time now..."

"You can buy dog carriers," Mum said, stroking one finger over Frankie's golden nose. "Special bags, with spaces for them to put their heads out. I saw a lady on the train with one the other day, a pink bag that looked just like a handbag, except there was a little white fluffy dog peering out of one end! I think she must have been taking her dog to work."

"That's mad," Dad muttered.

"You take Shadow and Frankie to work," Kitty pointed out, wishing her pockets were big enough to put Frankie in – she could just imagine a furry, squidgy pocketful of puppy.

"Yes, but I work at the kitchen table." Dad rolled his eyes. "I don't have a lot of choice. There are days when I'd love a nice quiet office. Particularly if Frankie gets all het up because he can see a cat out of the back door. Which he usually does just when I'm on the phone about something very important."

"You love him really," Mum said. "I think you enjoy moaning about him."

Kitty nodded. When they'd got Frankie a few weeks before, he was officially meant to be Mum's dog, but he adored Dad, partly because it was usually Dad who was at home to feed him and play with him while Kitty and Sam and Luke were at school. He liked to show Dad how much he loved him by chewing his shoes. Now Dad had started keeping all his shoes on a bookshelf that Frankie couldn't reach, so he just sat underneath it looking wistful instead. Dad had been really annoyed about the holes in his favourite pair of trainers – he'd even said he didn't know why they'd got another puppy – but Kitty had seen him later on typing on his laptop with one hand because Frankie had fallen asleep on his arm, so she was sure Dad hadn't meant it.

The rain was just starting as they got back to their road, and Kitty pulled her hood up and huddled her nose and chin inside her coat – the rain was icy, even though it was April already.

Everyone sped up, thinking how good it would be get inside.

"Bella!" She pulled her hand out of her pocket to wave as she spotted Bella and Oscar from next door just getting into their car. "Bella, you have to look at Frankie!"

Bella was almost exactly the same age as Kitty, and they'd been friends since before they were born, Mum said. She and Bella's mum had gone to classes at the baby clinic together, and compared notes about the size of their bumps and the weird things they'd felt like eating. Bella and Oscar had a cat and three guinea pigs, but no dog, and Bella adored Shadow and Frankie. Bella and Kitty were in the same class at school, and they hung out with each other a lot in the holidays.

"Where is he?" Bella looked round their feet, a confused expression on her face. Usually Frankie would bounce up to her to be fussed over.

Dad turned round so Bella could see his pocket, with Frankie perfectly positioned under the flap so the rain dripped straight off past his nose.

"Awww!" Bella squeaked. "I can't believe he fits in your pocket. It's like it was made for carrying him."

Kitty nodded. "I know. He's been asleep

all the way home. Maybe we should design a whole lot of clothes with puppy pockets, Bella. We could be millionaires. Frankie can be our official mascot."

Frankie wriggled suddenly and poked his nose out further, just in time to get a large raindrop right on the end. He gave a grumpy little yap and burrowed back into Dad's pocket, so they couldn't see any of him at all, just a fat round bulge under the shiny yellow coat.

Dad sighed. "Now he's probably never coming out."

Bella grinned at him. "You might have to get another coat; that one's Frankie's now."

Kitty nodded. "Definitely, Dad. You're not having it back. See you tomorrow, Bella!"

2

"A new girl? Really? That's weird, just in the middle of the term. Are you sure?"

"Absolutely sure." Bella nodded. "I was taking the register back to Mrs Marsh in the office, and she was there, with her mum. Mrs Marsh said I'd be in the same class. She's just moved here and she's called Erin."

"Did she look nice?" Kitty frowned. They hadn't had anyone new in their class for ages. Not since they'd been in Year 2, as far as she could remember. It would be really odd.

"I don't know." Bella shrugged, glancing at the others around their table. "I mean, she's really pretty. She had this amazing plait thing in her hair. Like a heart shape – it must have taken someone ages to do it before school. I didn't get to talk to her or anything though."

"You know what," Louisa whispered in Kitty's ear. "If she really is in our class, she's going to be on our table."

Kitty blinked. She hadn't thought of that. Their table only had the four of them – her, Bella, Louisa and Maisie – and they were all friends. They hung around together almost all the time, even though Kitty would have said Louisa was actually her best friend. They'd been sitting on this table since the beginning of Year 5, and they all just fitted together. Mr Bentley was always threatening to move people around, but somehow he never did. Louisa was right, though – there was definitely room for another person. They were the only table with four, apart from the boys up at the front right under Mr B's nose, and he'd never stick a new girl with them.

"I don't want a new girl," she whispered back.

"Me neither." Louisa made a face. "We'll have to look after her. Show her around. It'll be really boring."

Kitty leaned her chin on one hand and tried to look as though she was listening to Mr Bentley talk about uncountable nouns while she imagined going to a new school. She'd gone to toddler group with Bella and Louisa, and then on to the nursery that was part of their school. Same with Brownies and dancing, and all the other stuff they did. She'd always had lots of friends; it wasn't something she'd had to worry about. She actually couldn't think what it would be like, not to know *anyone*.

She peered around the room, trying to think what it would be like to walk in and have no idea what anyone in her class was like. Not to know that you shouldn't ever talk to Maisie in maths because she hated it so much it made her bad-tempered. Or that if Joshua was being really nice it was probably because he wanted something. *We could write her a guide*, Kitty thought, smiling to herself behind her hand. *Kitty and Louisa's Guide to 5B. Except if Maisie or Joshua or the others ever saw it they might think we were trying to be horrible. And then they'd tell. No, maybe better not. . .*

But she had persuaded herself that she ought to be nice to the new girl – nicer than she felt like being, anyway.

"My dad was working in Australia," Erin explained, looking around the lunch table in between bites of her wrap. "We've been there for two years. But now he's back with the office over here."

"Wow," Maisie murmured. "It must be really strange being back."

"It's cold." Erin shivered dramatically. "Freezing. It's autumn in Sydney now, so it's just nice – not too hot, but really sunny."

"Sydney..." Kitty sighed. It sounded so exotic. "I'd love to go there."

"It's great." Erin nodded. "It's nice being back

and seeing my grandma and my two granddads again though."

"Why didn't you go back to the school you were at before?" Louisa asked. Then she went red. "Not that we don't want you here! I just wondered."

"I thought I would," Erin said quietly. "But they were full. The head teacher said she was really sorry, she just couldn't do anything about it." Her shoulders slumped a little, and she stared at her lunch.

Louisa looked guilty. "Sorry..." There was a strange, uncomfortable silence while everyone tried to think what to say, and then Louisa said, "So, what do you like to do?" Her voice sounded too bouncy, a bit like someone's mum trying too hard, but Erin smiled at her gratefully. "I like dancing. And swimming. We used to go to the beach a lot."

Erin looked like the kind of person who was always on a beach, Kitty thought, feeling envious. She had beach-blonde hair, a bit wavy, and the top part of it was pulled up into that heart-shaped plait, which all the girls in their class were already trying to work out how to do. The rest of her hair was really long, almost down to her waist.

"What was your school like in Sydney?" Bella asked. "Did you have school uniform?"

"Yes." Erin grinned. "It's better here – we had to wear dresses all year, and they were yellow. Not even a nice yellow. Navy blue's a lot better, honestly. And you've got a bigger playground, I reckon. Is there a library? I like reading too."

Bella nodded. "It's tiny though."

"We'll show you when you've finished your lunch; we're allowed in there at lunchtime as long as we're quiet," Louisa explained.

"Oh, I'm done now." Erin zipped up her lunch bag, looking eager.

"OK, me too," Louisa agreed. Kitty was just about to say that she'd nearly finished, but the two of them were already gone, and she was left staring after them, her mouth still half open.

"Hi, Kitty! Where's Louisa?"

Kitty looked up from the daisy chain she was making and saw Maisie and Bella eyeing her. She shrugged a little. "Still showing Erin the library, I suppose." The grassy bank that made one side of their playground was one of their gang's favourite places. They often spent lunches chatting there, the four of them. She'd been making daisy chains, because she couldn't exactly sit there and do nothing. Probably she could have gone and joined in with the girls playing football on the other side of the playground – but they'd have looked at her just like Maisie and Bella were looking at her now...

"I thought you went after them?" Maisie asked.

She didn't want to tell Maisie what had happened. She'd caught up with Louisa and Erin, but somehow she just hadn't felt very welcome. Or even wanted. Erin had given her a sweet sort of smile and said it was fine, she didn't need both of them to show her the library.

"You go and play with somebody else!" she'd said, waving vaguely at the playground.

Go and play! As if Kitty was about five. But Louisa hadn't said anything, even though Kitty had stared at her, in a *What's going on?* sort of way. She'd been waiting for Louisa to say she should stay, but Louisa wouldn't catch her eye; she was just staring down the corridor. As if she was actually avoiding looking at Kitty.

It wasn't even fair – Mr B had told them both to look after Erin during lunch. But it was like Erin had just picked Louisa and left Kitty behind. If she said anything it would sound like she was making a fuss. *But Mr Bentley told both of us to show you stuff. . .* It would sound so whiny and babyish.

It'll be all right later, Kitty told herself firmly. Louisa was just being polite. Everything would be back to normal soon. Erin had had a whole morning to get to know the school, and it wasn't as if Whitehorse Primary was all that big. Erin had to have seen it all by now. After lunch, Erin would just be the new girl they had to be nice to. She'd be getting in the way a bit until she found some friends of her own. That was all.

Kitty smiled up at Maisie and Bella. "I just didn't feel like it." She shrugged. "Want to make daisy chains?" She wasn't sure they actually believed her – she saw them look at each other – but she smiled and smiled, and grabbed another fistful of daisies, and tried to convince herself that it was true.

"Are you OK, Kitty?" Dad looked down at her thoughtfully as he opened the front door and Sam and Luke stormed inside to make themselves some toast. "You didn't talk much on the way home."

Kitty nodded. She didn't feel like telling Dad

about her day. And if she said she was miserable, she'd have to explain why. "I'm OK. Just tired."

"All right. Want me to make you some toast too?"

"No thanks, Dad. I might go upstairs and read for a bit. Can I take Frankie?" Kitty hung up her jacket, and then turned at the clicking of claws to see Frankie hurrying out of the kitchen to meet them.

"Hello, you..." She crouched down, smiling at him. It felt like the first time she'd smiled all afternoon – the stiff, worried feeling went out of her face as Frankie bounced his paws on her knees and licked and sniffed and loved her.

He did love Sam and Luke too, but they were dancing around and stamping their feet and it was all just too noisy. Shadow was probably in his basket with his head under the cushion pretending to be asleep, Kitty reckoned.

"Do you want to come upstairs with me?" Kitty asked, scooping Frankie into her arms. He didn't wriggle or complain, just sniffed curiously at the outdoor scent of her, and then at the banisters and the photos on the walls up the stairs. He didn't go upstairs that often – the steps were too steep, and they were shiny polished wood. Frankie had tried scrabbling up them a couple of times, but Mum had told them to take him back downstairs again if they saw him. Dachshunds' long backs didn't work well with stairs, she explained. He could damage his spine if he tried to climb them. He wasn't even supposed to jump on to the sofa – which just meant that he went on the sofa all the time, because as soon as anybody saw him looking at it hopefully, they picked him up and put him there.

"I know, it's nice, isn't it?" Kitty murmured. "You are allowed, don't worry. It's just that Mum said we had to carry you. And then watch out to see if you wanted to go back downstairs because you needed a wee. You can help me take my mind off school, Frankie."

She put him down when they got to her bedroom, and Frankie set off round the room, sniffing into all the corners as he explored. "Don't eat that." Kitty whisked a piece of paper out from under his nose. "That's my homework. Mr Bentley wouldn't believe me if I said you'd eaten it."

She sat down with her back against the bed

and sighed. There was a photo of her and Louisa pinned up on the board above her desk. They were on the swings at the park by school, and Louisa's mum had taken it. She'd printed it out and given Kitty a copy because it was so nice – both of them swooping up into the air and laughing. It had only been a few weeks before, but now it felt as if it was years ago.

"Don't be silly," Kitty muttered to herself. "You're making something out of nothing." Mum said that a lot. She said that Kitty *liked* to worry. Maybe that was a little bit true, but not today. "Hello, Frankie." He'd finished sniffing every bit of her bedroom now. He stood next to her, looking up hopefully, and put a feathery little paw on her lap. "Come on then." Kitty patted her knees – she was cross-legged, and her school skirt stretched out made a sort of nest, perfectly dachshund-sized. Frankie curled up, and Kitty couldn't help smiling. He was too sweet, even if she was miserable.

"And I don't care that you're getting hairs all over my school skirt, either," she murmured. "I'll get them off with sticky tape." She ran her hand over his ears and tickled the creases in his tummy where he was folded up. "Do you think I'm boring?" she whispered to him. "Erin's so pretty. And she's new, and everything about her is different. Maybe that's why Louisa didn't talk to me all afternoon."

Frankie snorted and wriggled, and squidged himself firmly back into place. "OK, sorry. I won't tickle you." Kitty looked over at the photo again. "Why does she like Erin better than me? She's only known her a day!"

Frankie snorted again, and then wheezed gently. He was asleep. "Oh well. I suppose you weren't really listening anyway. . ."

Erin was funny, that was the problem, she decided. Funny and new, and that made her exciting. And she had a phone – a really smart one, with a camera, and she had apps on it to do things to the photos to make them look better. Or add stupid stuff to them. She'd taken one of Mr Bentley and then at the end of lunch she'd shown it to everyone with a moustache stuck on. Most of the girls in their class had been gathered round laughing at it. Kitty had tried to tell her to be careful, that if Mr Bentley caught her with a phone – let alone caught her taking photos in class – she'd be in real trouble. They weren't allowed to have them out in school.

Erin had just smiled at her cheekily. "How's he going to find out?" she asked. As if she thought Kitty was going to tell! And then everyone had stared at Kitty, as though she really might, and Erin and Louisa had turned their backs on her, giggling over the phone. Kitty felt her cheeks burn at the thought of it. They'd just left her standing there, all of them. She'd perched on the arm of the bench next to Bella, pretending she didn't care. It hadn't lasted long – Louisa had said something about the literacy they'd been working on together, and Kitty was back in the group again. But then all afternoon, Erin and Louisa had had their heads together, whispering and giggling. Kitty was almost sure that some of the time they'd been laughing at *her*. She wouldn't have told – of course she wouldn't.

3

"I know, you want to come too." Kitty rubbed Frankie's ears, and then ran her hand over the smooth dome of his head – it was so silky, she loved the feel of him. "You're just too little, Frankie. When you're bigger and you can walk faster, then you can."

Frankie put his paws on her knees and yapped excitedly – he could tell they were going out, and he was ever hopeful.

"Come on, Kitty. I can see Bella and Oscar waiting for us," Dad said, waiting impatiently by the front door and jangling his keys. "Sam! Luke! When I said put your lunch box in your bag, what do you think I meant? I can see them on the kitchen table! Hurry up, you lot! That's it. Make sure Frankie doesn't slip out behind you, Kitty. Bye, Frankie, be a good dog. No chewing!"

Kitty and Bella almost always walked to school together. Either Kitty's dad took them, or Bella's mum, and then they'd swap for the walk home. The school was only a few minutes' walk away, but there were busy roads to cross.

Kitty had tried asking if she and Bella could walk on their own, but one of their parents had to be around anyway – there was no way that Sam and Luke and Oscar would be allowed to go by themselves, and their older sisters didn't want to have to be in charge of them, either. But they usually got to walk either ahead of the others or a way behind, so it almost felt as though they were on their own.

"Did you start that history homework?" Bella asked as they wandered along the next morning. "It was really hard, making all those notes."

"Mmm. . ." Kitty said vaguely. She'd tried, but the homework was research for their topic, and ancient Chinese gods just hadn't seemed very important the night before. She hadn't been able to get what had been going on at school out of her mind enough to concentrate, and her notes were so messy they looked like Frankie had made most of them.

"Are you OK?" Bella asked after a while. "You're not saying much."

"I'm fine. Just tired." Kitty tried to smile at

her, but she felt miserable. If Bella had noticed that she was feeling upset, then everybody else would. There was no way she wanted Louisa and Erin – *especially* Erin – thinking that she cared. She felt as though the top of her skin had been rubbed off, and all of her was soft and stinging. Every word hurt.

They walked on in silence again, and Kitty kicked at bits of gravel and worried about what today was going to be like. It was so unfair – and it seemed even more unfair because she'd never expected anything like this to happen to her. *It might be fine*, she thought. *Maybe it was just a first-day thing. Now that Louisa's got used to Erin being around, she'll be back to being my friend again. Maybe I should ask her about it? But what if she says she doesn't like me any more?*

"Erin's nice, isn't she?" Bella said suddenly.

"What?" Kitty snapped, shocked out of being polite.

"I just said that I think Erin's nice. She's funny. And I wish I had a phone like that. I asked Mum if I could have one for my birthday and she said no way, not until I'm going to secondary school and walking by myself. That's such a long time."

"I don't think her phone's that special," Kitty growled. "It's just a phone. So what."

Bella stared at her. "But it does all that cool stuff. And she can take brilliant photos."

"Honestly, Bella, you sound like you're about three. 'She can take brilliant photos!' Photos aren't so special! Sometimes you're such a baby, I don't even know why I'm friends with you!"

Kitty heard the words coming out of her mouth – she was sure she hadn't decided to say them. They just seemed to happen, and then they were there, floating in the air between her and Bella. Between her and Bella's shocked, hurt face. Bella had huge blue eyes anyway, and now they were huger and bluer and rounder than ever, and shining with tears.

Kitty wanted to take back what she'd said at once. It was just that she was angry with Erin and Louisa; she knew quite well none of it was Bella's fault.

Well, except Bella could have stuck up for her yesterday, and then not been so excited about Erin and her phone... Anyway. It wasn't Bella's fault, so it wasn't fair to shout at her.

She definitely hadn't meant to make Bella cry. Had she?

The thing was, now that Bella was standing there, sniffing, with tears just about to spill over and run down her face, and the edges of her eyes and nose going all red, like a white rabbit, there was a tiny part of Kitty that wanted her to stay that way. Most of her was desperate to say sorry and make it up, but the small, mean, angry bit of her was enjoying watching Bella try not to cry. It made her feel better about all those moments the day before, when she'd felt so left out. Making Bella miserable somehow made Kitty forget how unhappy *she* was.

Determinedly, Kitty squashed down the mean part of her, way down deep inside. "I didn't mean it," she said hurriedly. "I'm sorry, Bella. Of course we're friends, you know we are. I'm just—"

"That was a really mean thing to say," Bella faltered. She was still crying, and there were bright pink circles on her cheeks now too. "I'm not a baby – just because I don't go round saying horrible things to people!"

For a tiny moment, Kitty thought about snarling something back, as if Bella had deserved it and she didn't know how horrible Kitty could be if she really tried. Because then Bella would be crying for real, and Kitty wouldn't be the only one feeling so lonely and strange. But she didn't. Instead she stared at her feet, muttering, "Sorry. Really sorry, Bella. I'm in a stupid mood, that's all."

Bella stared at her, and then rubbed her eyes and set off walking again, hurrying after Kitty's dad and the boys, who were nearly at the end of the road.

4

By the time they got to school, Bella was almost back to normal. Kitty had done her best to cheer her up, telling her about Frankie bouncing through the grass on Sunday afternoon. She'd even acted it out, and Bella had laughed so much that her pink face and teary eyes could almost be put down to that. Certainly that was what Dad thought, when Kitty and Bella finally caught up with the others and Bella was still giggling.

"I was telling her about Frankie – the way his ears flapped when he was bouncing," Kitty explained.

Dad smiled. "How does a dog so small have ears like that? I think he nicked them off someone bigger."

"They get in everything," Sam agreed. "Mum reckons we should clip them back when he's eating, Bella." He nudged Luke. "Remember that special puppy porridge?"

Bella and Oscar stared. "Puppy porridge? Dogs can't eat porridge. . ." Oscar said doubtfully.

"Dogs can eat anything. Anything they can get their paws on. Oh, except chocolate," Dad added. "It's poisonous for dogs. Dark chocolate is, anyway, the kind I like."

"It's poisonous to me too." Kitty shuddered. "I can't stand it. It doesn't even taste like chocolate."

Dad smiled rather smugly. "Well, I happen to like it very much. And nobody in the family ever wants me to share it. It's quite lucky really."

"Frankie used to have porridge when we first got him," Kitty explained to Bella, waving goodbye to Dad as they headed into the playground and he set off home. "It's got lots of vitamins, I think."

"When Frankie's a bit bigger, do you think your dad will bring him on the walk to school?" Bella asked.

"Maybe. He didn't used to bring Shadow because he said he needed to have his hands free for Sam and Luke, but maybe now they're bigger we can bring the dogs. Or just Frankie – Shadow's legs hurt when he walks too much on hard pavements. Bringing Frankie would be fab, once he can walk fast enough." Kitty sat down on one of the benches, smiling at the thought. She loved taking Frankie for walks – he made everyone so happy to see him, and people were always telling her how gorgeous he was. She waved as Maisie and Louisa came across the playground, and tried to ignore the sudden squirming in her stomach. Would Louisa say anything about the day before?

But she didn't – she was just like always, and Kitty's odd, sicky feeling died away. Louisa had been playing netball for the school team after school the day before, and she was really excited about it. They'd won by miles, which had never happened before.

"I actually scored two goals," she said, grinning delightedly. "And Josie Matthews in Year 6 – she's the captain—"

"We know," Maisie put in. "You *might* have told us that before."

"Sorry! I'm excited!"

"It's all right," Bella said soothingly. "What did Josie Matthews do?"

"She said I was the MVP," Louisa said blissfully. "That means Most Valuable Player. That's going to be announced in assembly." She glanced over Kitty's shoulder and waved. "Hey, Erin!"

Erin waved back, and came to stand next to Louisa. Kitty felt her stomach jump again, but Louisa was still gabbling on about the netball match.

"And we even got a medal, because it was a qualifier for some sort of league thing." She pulled it out of her bag and waved it triumphantly at them.

"You're so lucky," Bella sighed. "I wish I could be on a team."

"Really?" Kitty looked at her, surprised. "You've got dancing medals though."

"I know." Bella shrugged. "But it would be nice to be part of a school team. No one's going to announce my dance medals in assembly, are they?"

"Which ones have you got?" Erin asked. "Do you do ballet exams?"

"Mm-hm, and tap. That's my favourite." Bella smiled at her.

"I love tap!" Erin looked excited. "Where do you go? Mum says she's going to find me a new dancing school, but she hasn't yet. It would be great to go with somebody I know."

The bell rang, and Bella and Erin grabbed

their bags and went on talking about dancing as they headed across the playground to the door. Kitty bit down hard on her bottom lip, trying not to panic. Not Bella too!

Kitty sort of knew that she wasn't being fair. Erin was only being friendly, and so was Bella. She didn't need to get jealous. It was just that now Louisa and Maisie were talking netball again, and Kitty couldn't think of anything to say to Erin and Bella about dancing. Even now they were in the classroom they were still talking about tap and ballet and how hard the exams were. Kitty was just sitting there fiddling with the stuff in her pencil case feeling like she didn't belong. Now that Erin was on their table too, everything seemed to be different.

"Are you going to show your medal to Mr Bentley?" Bella leaned over to Louisa. "You should."

Louisa looked pleased. "Maybe. I don't want to sound like I'm making a big fuss about it..."

"You won't!" Bella nudged her. "It's special, you should definitely get him to show everyone. Mr Bentley! Look what Louisa's got!" She waved at him.

"Stop showing off," Kitty hissed across the corner of the table at her, as Mr Bentley came over from the whiteboard to admire the medal and then hold it up for everyone to see.

"I'm not!" Bella stared at her in surprise. "How can I be showing off; it's not even my medal!"

"You're always sucking up to Mr Bentley," Kitty whispered.

Bella ducked her head, staring down at the table. *Obviously* she was going to cry again, Kitty thought, watching. She was a bit scared that Mr Bentley would notice and she'd get into trouble, but he was telling everyone how proud they should be of Louisa, and how important it was to work as a team. She glanced quickly at the others. Had they seen her being horrible? Louisa and Maisie hadn't noticed; they were watching everyone admire Louisa's medal. But Erin was looking straight at her, Kitty realized, a little uneasily. So now the new girl probably thought she was mean – and she *was*. Why was she being like this? Kitty stared down at her pencils again, feeling guilty, and confused, and completely miserable.

★

Bella hardly spoke to Kitty on the way home. Luckily, Oscar was furious about something his class teacher had done that was totally unfair and he was making such a fuss that Bella's mum didn't notice how silent the girls were.

Kitty kept stealing glances at Bella's pink eyes, and wondering how Bella felt. *She* had made her look like that. That was awful. But at the same time, Erin and Louisa had both laughed when she put felt tip freckles on Bella's cheek during their silent reading. Everyone had liked her then. Louisa was still her friend, even if Erin seemed to be in on everything now as well. Anyway, she hadn't done anything *really* mean. She'd only told Bella the truth. She *did* suck up to Mr Bentley. And the felt tip thing was only a joke. Bella was just being sensitive, Kitty told herself. She needed to toughen up.

But it was odd, watching Bella disappear into her garden without even saying goodbye. She could hear Bella's mum asking her if she was all right as she opened the front door. Kitty strained her ears – Bella just said something about wanting a drink. It was OK then – Bella wasn't going to tell. Kitty sucked in a deep, relieved breath and waved at Dad, who was standing at the front door.

Frankie peeped over the edge of Shadow's basket as Kitty and Sam and Luke came into the kitchen. He had his own basket – dachshund-sized – but he didn't like it very much. He definitely preferred squeezing into Shadow's with him instead. Shadow groaned as Frankie wriggled and then jumped hard on his stomach to get out of the basket. He lay there, looking humble and long-suffering while Frankie danced round the children, whining with excitement.

"Poor old Shadow," Kitty murmured, rubbing his velvety black ears. "You're so good. You're such a nice dog." She sat down next to his basket and sighed as he rested his heavy muzzle on her knee. He really was good, she thought uncomfortably. He put up with Frankie bossing him about all the time, and he didn't seem to mind that the little dog got all the fussing because he was new and sweet and cuddly. "Maybe dogs are just nicer than people," Kitty said, leaning over and whispering into Shadow's ear. "Do you think so? You never

ever do anything to Frankie, even when he steals your basket and jumps on your tummy. I'm not nearly as nice as you, Shadow. I've been so mean, all day." She swallowed, and sniffed hurriedly.

Kitty stood in the middle of the corridor, watching. She knew she was somewhere familiar. School? It looked sort of school-like – there were doors here and there. But no noticeboards or anything like that. Just a long, long grey corridor, and an awful sense that something was wrong. Kitty took a step forward, and then another and another, and then she found herself running, chasing after a small figure right at the other end of the grey corridor. She was running as fast as could, but even as she ran, she knew that it wouldn't be fast enough. She was too late, even though she didn't know what she was late for. She pounded her feet against the greyish floor, trying to be quicker. She couldn't give up. She mustn't. She knew – without understanding *how* she knew – that it was important. More important than anything else.

The tiny figure at the end of the corridor turned and looked at her. It wasn't very clear. Just a thin person in a green jumper, like their school uniform. A thin person with a pale face, and pale hair. A bit pinkish round the eyes. Bella.

Kitty set her teeth and pumped her arms and raced faster down the corridor, but the pale girl turned back and walked away through the door at the end of the passage. Kitty was too late...

Kitty woke up, clawing at the duvet, trying to struggle free so that she could keep running. She'd pushed the whole duvet on to the floor by the time she realized that it had been a dream.

Shivering, she hauled the duvet back, and sat curled up against the wall. "I don't even know what that was about," she whispered to herself. "But it was horrible."

Her door opened, and Mum came in, her face worried in the light from the landing. "Did you have a bad dream, Kitty love? I heard you shouting."

"Yes..." Kitty said shakily, wondering if she could tell Mum what it was about. She did want to – sort of. She wanted Mum to tell her it was all going to be OK. But she couldn't tell her mum how awful she'd been to Bella. She was ashamed.

"What were you dreaming about?" Mum asked, giving her a hug.

"I – I can't remember," Kitty whispered.

"Poor you. I know." Mum smiled. "Wait a minute." She went out, and Kitty heard her hurrying downstairs, and then coming back up again. "You couldn't have a bad dream with Frankie on your bed, could you?" she said, snuggling the sleepy puppy into a little nest of Kitty's duvet. "Not for the whole night, Kitty, just for a little bit. I'll come and get him when I go to bed, and put him back in the kitchen. Sleep well – dream about Frankie this time!"

Kitty nodded. "Thanks, Mum." She stroked

Frankie's ears, and he made a sleepy little grunting noise. He *was* making her feel better.

"It wasn't real," she whispered to him as she lay down again. "Dreams don't mean anything. It isn't too late. I'll be nice to Bella tomorrow. Really, really nice."

5

Kitty tried. She really did. She was as nice as she could possibly be for the whole walk to school. Bella didn't even say hello when she and her mum and Oscar turned up at the front door. Bella's mum glanced worriedly between them, as though she knew that something was wrong, but she didn't say anything. Bella kept trying to walk as far away from Kitty as she could, but Kitty followed her, chattering frantically about homework and Frankie and Shadow and how Maisie's mum had said she could have a party at the ice rink and plans for half-term next week and everything she could possibly think of. It took half of the walk to school before Bella even smiled. Once they got into the playground and she was safely away from her mum, she turned on Kitty and said flatly, "Why are you being so nice now, when you were mean to me all of yesterday?"

"No, I wasn't. . ." Kitty tried to look surprised, but she had a feeling it wasn't very convincing.

"Drawing on my face?" Bella snapped. "Did you just forget about that?"

"It was a joke!" Kitty shrugged as innocently as she could. "It was funny, Bella. I wasn't trying to be mean."

"Yeah, right," Bella muttered, but she didn't say anything more, and Kitty knew that she was going to let it go.

"Hi, Bella! Hi, Kitty!" Erin came in through

the gate, waving at them, and Kitty felt a tightness in her throat. She'd spent so much time last night worrying about how horrible she'd been to Bella, she'd almost forgotten about Erin. But at least Erin was talking to them – she wasn't going to pretend Kitty didn't exist, like she had that first day.

"Did you bring them?" Erin asked Bella, and Bella nodded, pink and pleased.

"Yes, all of them. Do you want to see?"

"What is it?" Kitty peered over as Bella swung her rucksack off her back and started to dig around inside.

"My dancing medals. Erin wanted to see them," Bella explained, pulling out a pink drawstring bag with a little mouse in a tutu embroidered on it. "Oh – my gran gave me this ages ago," she added, looking a bit embarrassed. "I know it's a bit babyish."

"It's sweet," Erin said, and Kitty folded her lips together so as not to say anything – because she *had* been thinking the bag was babyish.

Bella pulled out a handful of medals. They were actually beautiful – some on different coloured ribbons, with pictures of dancers in the middle of some of them, and some attached to pin badges – but what was impressive was that there were so many.

"Oh, I've got that one." Erin fingered a gold medal with a pair of ballet shoes embossed on to it. "You've got loads though. Have you been dancing for ever, Bella?"

Bella beamed at her. "I was two when I first went to ballet. Oh, Miss Adams is over there – I'm just going to show them to her." She hurried across the playground, waving at the student who was teaching all their PE lessons this term, and leaving Kitty and Erin staring at each other.

"So are you going to Bella's dance school too?" Kitty asked, for something to say. She couldn't just stand there and say nothing, not with Erin looking at her like that.

"Maybe." Erin smiled at her. "Did you like the medals?"

Kitty shrugged. "I suppose so – they're pretty. I'm not really into dancing though. I did go to gymnastics for a bit, but now I just do swimming."

"Hi, Kitty!" Louisa came running over. She looked pleased to see Kitty – but surprised at the same time. Kitty felt a strange sort of sinking in her stomach. Louisa had wanted to talk to Erin, not to her... It was going to be like the other day, when they went off together and left her alone.

Erin was admiring Louisa's hair, and Kitty realized that she had the same kind of hairdo that Erin had on the first day she'd come. Louisa had French plaits pulled into a sort of crown shape round the top of her head – she'd never done her hair like that before. It looked really pretty, and it must have taken ages. Kitty sighed to herself. She liked her hair – it was fair and straight and thick, and she'd never bothered growing it long. It was too much fuss having to tie it back for school. She hadn't minded not having long hair, until now.

"It's really pretty," Erin told Louisa. "You should show Bella how to do it – it looks like it would be good for dancing. She's over there, showing her dancing medals to Miss Adams."

Kitty pressed her fingernails into her palms – more dancing. "She's showing them off because you had your netball medal yesterday," she muttered. Then she realized that Erin and Louisa were both staring at her.

"Are you jealous?" Louisa asked curiously – she was looking at Kitty with her head on one side, like Kitty was some sort of strange beast in a zoo.

"No! Of course not! They're just medals, who cares!" Kitty said it without really thinking – she was wishing they could talk about something she liked for once.

"Didn't you mean all those things you said yesterday about my netball medal then?" Louisa asked coldly. Her eyes were narrowed. Louisa had never looked at her like that before, Kitty thought. Louisa was supposed to be her best friend.

"No! I mean – yes! Ohhh..." Kitty sighed. "Bella's just going on and on about them, that's all. I mean, look at her." She glanced across the playground, and then back at Louisa and Erin, almost begging them to understand, and laugh with her. "She's showing half the teachers! It's just a bit ... I don't know..."

Erin and Louisa exchanged a look, and Erin said, "Actually, Bella's worked really hard to get all those."

"You really are jealous, Kitty." Louisa gave

her a pitying look, and the two of them walked away from her together as the bell went.

Kitty sat in the hall, tearing bits off her sandwiches. She wasn't hungry. She'd hung around with the others at break, like she usually did, but she was sure Louisa wasn't really talking to her, and Bella was definitely avoiding her too. Louisa was talking to Erin about getting her mum to take them shopping together in the holidays. Kitty wanted to scream, *Why aren't you asking me?*

Things seemed to be getting worse and worse – Kitty felt like she had a handful of sand, slipping through her fingers. She had to *do* something!

Louisa started to talk to Maisie about something, and Erin leaned over to Kitty. "Are you OK, Kitty?" she murmured, so the others couldn't hear. "What's the matter?"

Kitty stared at her in surprise. "Nothing," she mumbled. She was hardly going to say *You've stolen my best friend and now no one likes me any more*, but that was how she felt.

"OK." Erin shrugged, and went back to talking to Louisa on her other side.

Kitty watched her furiously, hating her

perfect hair, and her coolness, and that stupid phone and the way she'd just walked in and stolen everything.

Slowly, she squashed the rest of her lunch back into her box. She didn't want it. Her stomach was turning over. She didn't want to be in the hall with everyone else either – everybody talking and laughing was making her feel more and more lonely. And it would be just the same out in the playground. They weren't supposed to be in the classrooms at lunchtime, but maybe she could sneak in and read a book or something? No one would notice, would they?

She wandered back towards their classroom, thinking about what excuse she could use if anyone caught her. "I've lost something," she muttered. They had PE after lunch. "Lost my trainers – I had to take them home and I can't remember if I brought them back. OK." She peered through the glass panel in the classroom door. It didn't look like Mr Bentley was in there. Kitty slipped round the door, her heart thumping. She wasn't used to doing things wrong.

Kitty hurried over to their table, meaning to get her book, and then find somewhere to sit out of the way. Perhaps by the coats? Mr Bentley wouldn't notice her there, if he came back. She grabbed her rucksack, accidentally bumping it against Bella's. Something clattered on to the floor, and Kitty leaned down to pick it up. That cutesy little pink bag. Bella's medals, that she'd been going on and on about all day. Kitty's fingers tightened on it slowly...

She could see Bella outside in the playground

with Maisie – she was laughing, and she didn't look anything like the sad little figure in Kitty's dream. But Kitty knew it had been her. And she knew how much it would hurt Bella if she did something awful like taking those medals. Not just because they were precious, but because she was supposed to be Bella's friend. *I am Bella's friend*, she told herself firmly.

She still wanted to take them, though... She wanted to make somebody else as unhappy as she felt.

Kitty stood there with the bag in her hand, looking helplessly around the classroom. What was she going to do with them, anyway? She couldn't just put them in her own bag – what if someone saw them? Or Mr Bentley made everyone turn their bags out?

There was a noise suddenly outside the classroom, and Kitty gasped. She couldn't be caught with the bag in her hands. She stuffed it quickly down to the bottom of Maisie's satchel, under her cardigan, and hurried to the door. Whoever it was who'd made the noise had gone – they must have been just passing by. Kitty looked round the door and then slid out, feeling awful. Like a thief. But she wasn't really, was she? She hadn't actually stolen the medals, she told herself. Just moved them, that was all. Maybe Bella would think that she'd put them in the wrong bag. Kitty's stomach twisted again as she thought about it. She wished she'd never gone into the classroom at all. She hadn't meant to get anyone into trouble. She just wanted Louisa to be her friend again.

6

An hour later, Kitty was staring at her hands, wondering how she could ever have been so stupid. Bella was up at the front of the class with Mr Bentley, crying so much she couldn't even talk. Any minute now, Kitty was sure, they were going to have to empty out their bags. No one was going to believe that Maisie had taken the medals. Kitty didn't even want them to – she didn't want to get Maisie into trouble.

"All right." Mr Bentley sighed. "I'm sure this is just a misunderstanding. Can everyone please just check their bags and see if Bella's dancing medals have ended up in there by accident?"

A few of the boys snorted with laughter – dancing medals! But everyone started to look through their bags. Kitty picked up her rucksack. Of course she knew that the medals weren't in there, but she couldn't tell Mr Bentley that, could she? Out of the corner of her eye she watched Maisie pulling stuff out of her satchel. Kitty could see the exact moment when she found the medals. Her mouth actually dropped open. Kitty watched her, wondering what she'd do next. But Maisie didn't seem to worry about getting into trouble, or Bella thinking she might have taken the medals. She just waved them in the air and squeaked, "Bella, it's OK! They're here, I've got them!" And then Bella rushed at her and hugged her, and Erin and Louisa were hugging her too, and they were all laughing.

Kitty just watched them. All of a sudden she felt so lonely. She didn't belong with anybody now. Not even Bella, who'd always been so nice, and so loyal and friendly. She was the one who'd got Bella in that state. If Louisa wanted to be friends with Erin more than her, she should have let her. Instead she'd slipped into this awful game, and now she didn't have any friends at all. Bella was already sick of her being mean, and she didn't even know it was Kitty who'd taken the medals.

"So what happened then?" Mr Bentley asked. He sounded relieved. "Did you put them in the wrong bag, Bella? Do you two have bags that look the same, by any chance?"

Bella and Maisie exchanged doubtful looks, and showed him – Bella's pink rucksack, and

Maisie's silver satchel. There was no way anyone could mix those up. Mr Bentley sighed. "No... So." He looked around the table. "Any ideas, girls?"

Erin took a gasping breath, and looked up at him, and then across at Kitty. "Um... No..."

"What is it?" Mr Bentley looked impatient for a moment, but then Kitty saw him remember that Erin was new. "Have you thought of something, Erin?"

"It's just ... Kitty was in the classroom at lunchtime. But it can't have been Kitty – she's Bella's friend."

Kitty felt her cheeks burn. She couldn't tell if Erin was being mean on purpose or not. Bella was staring at her across the table, and everyone else in the class was peering round nosily, trying to eavesdrop on what was going on.

"I only came in because I thought I'd forgotten my trainers for PE," Kitty said. She wasn't sure if she sounded as though she was telling the truth or not. She wasn't used to having to lie – she'd never done anything like this before. She could feel tears burning her eyes.

"Well, all I can say is, girls, I'm disappointed that someone would do something so nasty in this class." Mr Bentley eyed them all. "I don't know what's been going on this week, but I haven't liked some of the behaviour on this table. Be careful, please, or I'll have to split you up. Bella, you'd better put those away safely, and I don't think we should be bringing precious things to school in future."

Bella nodded, but then she went back to staring at Kitty.

She knew.

At *least it's the holidays*, Kitty thought miserably as she slung her bag over her shoulder and trailed out of the cloakroom. *All I've got to do is get home without talking to Bella, somehow, and then I can hide in my room all week. Me and Frankie, we'll just huddle up.* She'd been a bit disappointed when Mum and Dad had told them they weren't going to stay with Gran, because Mum had so much work on. But now she was glad. She just wanted to stay in bed for the whole holiday – although there was no way Dad would actually let her. Not without hassling her about what was going on, anyway. . .

She looked over at the gates, wondering how long she could take to cross the playground and so avoid Bella as much as possible, and then she spotted Mum. Mum was there – and Dad. And Bella's mum and dad.

Kitty's heart jumped into her throat again, and she stopped in the middle of the playground. Mr Bentley must have called Mum and Dad. She was in trouble. Everybody knew what she'd done.

But then Sam raced up to her and grabbed her arm. "Come on! It's a surprise, hurry up, they won't tell us unless we're all there!"

Kitty felt as though the huge lump in her throat shrank just a little. Enough to get air round, anyway. She breathed in shakily. Sam was right – Mum and Dad were smiling, and chatting with Bella's parents. Dad was even holding Frankie tucked under his arm. They didn't look like people who'd just been told their daughter was a thief, or a bully.

"There you are!" Mum gave her a hug.

"What are you all doing here?" Kitty asked, stroking Frankie's ears and trying to sound normal. Bella was standing next to her mum – as far away from Kitty as she could get.

Dad beamed at her. "Surprise!"

"Tell us!" Luke and Sam and Oscar wailed.

"OK." Bella's dad pulled out his phone and showed them a photo – a house with a river running along in front of it. It looked beautiful.

"What is it?" Oscar demanded. "We're not moving house, are we?"

"No, you twit." His dad hugged one arm

round his shoulders. "We're all going on holiday there. All of us, both families together!"

"Isn't that a brilliant surprise?" Mum asked. "None of you suspected anything; we booked it months ago. We were going to tell you tomorrow, but then I realized I didn't want to do all of your packing and then have you complaining the whole week because I'd brought the wrong things."

"So what do you think?" It was Bella's mum who asked, but all four of them were looking round hopefully.

"Brilliant! Are your dogs coming?" Oscar asked Sam.

"I don't know! Are they?" Sam looked at Dad.

"Yes, though Frankie might have to stay home for some of the walks – this cottage is in

Wales, there's lot of beautiful places to go and explore, but he's a bit little."

"Bella, aren't you excited?" her mum asked. "You haven't said anything. Oh! Bella, what's the matter?"

Bella was holding her rucksack in front of her with her arms wrapped round it, as if she was scared someone was going to take it away, and she was crying.

*

Mum turned round from the window and sighed. "Look, Kitty, I know you and Bella have had something go wrong at school." She took a deep breath, and closed her eyes for a moment. It was what she did when she was really cross and she was trying not to snap. "But we're in this beautiful cottage, and we've been planning this trip for ages. I'm not going to let you spoil this holiday for the rest of the family."

"I'm not!" Kitty stared at her. "I haven't done anything!"

"Exactly," her dad muttered. "You're wandering around like a wet weekend, refusing to join in with everyone else. And you won't even talk to Bella!"

"I can't," Kitty whispered. "You don't understand. And Bella wouldn't talk to me if I did, either."

"What happened, Kitty?" her mum asked. "It can't have been that bad."

"Yes, it can," Kitty told her. "I can't say. I'm going upstairs." She darted out of the room before either of them could tell her not to, and for once, they didn't call her back. She let herself out of the back door into the garden, looking around for Frankie and wondering where all the others were too. Bella was probably in her room, reading or practising dance steps, so that was OK, but Kitty didn't want Sam and Luke and Oscar either. They were just too silly – nothing worried them and they bounced around all over the place making up mad songs and telling each

87

other the same jokes over and over again in different voices. Usually she didn't mind – she'd have Bella, and they could be the big sisters together. But now she was all on her own.

The cottage was on a hill, and all of the garden was a slope, with steps leading up to different bits, and a stream that ran twisting down between clumps of rocks and led to the river at the bottom of the hill. It was beautiful, and the weather was so good, it should have been the best holiday ever. But her parents were right – Kitty was spoiling it. Maybe not for the boys, but she knew Mum and Dad weren't happy. She couldn't do anything though, Kitty thought wearily as she picked her way up the slippery steps. She wasn't sure if she and Bella would talk to each other ever again. Maybe in years and years? Kitty sniffed, feeling suddenly lost. It wasn't until she couldn't be friends with Bella any more that she realized how much she missed her.

She stopped suddenly, hearing voices further up the garden. There were big rocks scattered around the banks of the stream that made good places to sit – were the boys playing by the stream further up the slope? She was hidden by a clump of tall bushes, so they wouldn't have seen her. She'd go somewhere else. Kitty was just turning to go back down when she realized that it was Bella, not the boys. She was talking to someone, almost whispering, and Kitty couldn't hear anyone answering back. But then she heard a scrabble of claws and a tiny yap, and she knew who Bella was with. Frankie. The garden had a stone wall around it, so the dogs were allowed outside, but they had to be careful to watch where they were – some of the parts of the wall had stones missing, or bits fallen down.

Even Frankie wanted someone else instead of her. *It's not as if he's her dog*, Kitty thought miserably, threading her way through the bushes so that she was well hidden in the middle. *It isn't fair. I wanted him.* But two minutes ago she'd been wishing she was still friends with Bella. Kitty sighed. Ever since Erin turned up at school, Kitty seemed to have been changing how she felt about things, backwards and forwards over and over again. Kitty wished she was friends with Bella again – but she couldn't see how it was ever going to happen. She hunched up silently as she heard Bella go past – she was carrying Frankie, as he couldn't climb down the steep steps.

"You're such a good dog," she heard Bella murmur. "I wish you were mine. I bet I'd look after you a lot better than Kitty."

Kitty flinched. Maybe Bella was right. She turned back to gaze through the bushes at the glint of water, wishing she could just run after them and say she was sorry.

7

"It'll be great." Kitty's dad had on his special super-enthusiastic voice, the one he used when he was jollying people along. It usually meant he wanted to do something like visiting a train museum, or making pasta from scratch – or going on a really long walk. "Honestly, I've looked it up – most of the route's along the side of the river, and there's a waterfall that's supposed to be spectacular. You'll love it."

Kitty sighed to herself. Usually, she did love Dad's walks. She was the one who persuaded Sam and Luke when they said they were tired, or they wanted to play on the computer and they couldn't be bothered. But not today. She couldn't get excited, even for a waterfall, and she loved them. The river was so gorgeous, she even knew Dad would let them splash around, and Shadow would go in too; it would be brilliant. Shadow's joints were loads better now the weather was warmer, and he was loving the walks. But everything seemed like too much effort when she felt so lonely. Plus she'd have to think about where Bella was the whole time, so that they could avoid each other.

"What about Frankie?" she asked. "He can't do a five-mile walk. Especially not along the riverbank, climbing over stones and stuff."

Dad frowned. "No, I suppose not... Well, we can carry him. I can put him in my coat pocket again if he gets tired."

Kitty's mum shook her head. "You don't want to wear a coat today; it's roasting. And actually, I think Kitty's right. Frankie's going to get too hot and tired going on a long walk today. You all go. I'll stay here with him. I'm not going to come with you; I've got a really spectacular pudding to make for dinner tonight."

"I'll stay too then," Kitty said quickly. "I'll play with him in the garden. He won't want to be shut up in the house, and he can't go in the garden if you're too busy cooking to keep an eye on him, Mum."

"OK." Dad looked disappointed, but he nodded. "Everyone else coming for a walk?"

Kitty watched as they packed up water bottles, and Sam's fishing net, and plasters because Luke always fell over wherever they went, and she almost wished she was going too. But then she thought of the garden, and Frankie to cuddle, with no one telling her to cheer up, or asking her why she wasn't being nice to Bella.

The bit of the garden that ran round in front of the cottage, just next to the road, was the only part that was actually flat. There was a tiny paved patio at the back, but after that the garden was in small flat bits dug out of the hill alongside the stream. Mostly Kitty thought the front garden was a bit boring, but it did have a swing seat, a wooden one with stripy cushions. Swinging there, with Frankie snuggled up on her knee, sounded exactly right for today.

"Frankie! Come on." Kitty clicked her fingers, and Frankie shot his head up out of Shadow's basket eagerly. He had been sulking in there, looking tiny all on his own. He hated it when Shadow got to go out and he didn't. He barked and launched himself over the edge of the basket, bouncing at Kitty and wagging his feathery tail. Kitty giggled. If he could talk, he'd be going, "Yes? Yes? What is it? Where are we going? What are we doing? Now, now, now!"

"You don't want to go and sit and rock, do you?" Kitty said, crouching down to rub his ears and make a fuss of him while he barked and jumped up at her knees and wagged so hard he shook all over. "Where's your ball? Where's the ball, Frankie? We'll wear you out a bit first."

Frankie ran right round the basket, squeaking with excitement, and then burrowed underneath the cushion part. He backed out again, looking a bit hot and bothered, and danced up and down in front of Kitty with a tennis ball in his mouth. Obviously he had taken his ball to bed with him.

"Come on then." Kitty let him out into the front garden and threw the ball. She had to be careful, since the garden wasn't huge, and it was next to the road – although the road was more of a lane. There were hardly any cars, since the cottage was a long way away from anywhere else.

Frankie chased backwards and forwards after the ball at top speed, and Kitty watched him, laughing and feeling better than she had in days. The tennis ball was twice as big as Frankie's muzzle, and he had to have his mouth wide open to hold it. Every so often he'd launch himself into the air for a catch, and he almost seemed to hover in the air. He'd drop down looking so proud of himself with his jaws stretched round the ball.

Then all at once he stopped, practically in mid-air, and he tensed up all over, staring curiously at the gate.

Kitty looked round and saw Bella fiddling with the latch, and then shoving the sticky gate open.

"What are you doing here?" Kitty asked sharply. She had been so enjoying the time with Frankie, not even thinking about Bella and the others. Now it all came surging back, and she remembered how awful she had been. It almost hurt to think about it.

"I twisted my ankle on the stones," Bella said. "I had to come back; I couldn't keep walking on it. We weren't that far – my dad walked with me till we could see the cottage and then he went back with the others."

Frankie dropped the ball and went to scrabble at Bella's knees, yipping at her happily. He obviously liked her so much, Kitty thought miserably, as she watched Bella fuss over him and whisper compliments to him. Then Frankie dashed away to fetch his ball, and carried it back to Bella, and Kitty snapped. She couldn't bear it. Frankie was her dog! Why should he want Bella to play with him, when Bella had spoiled everything?

"Frankie, no!" Kitty yelled. "No, leave it!" She raced over, grabbing the ball and trying to tug it away from him.

"What are you doing?" Bella gasped. "Don't

be so mean. Why can't he play with me if he wants to?"

"Don't tell me what to do with my dog!" Kitty hissed at her furiously. "Why do you have to ruin everything? You shouldn't even be here! This is meant to be my family's holiday, and you just muscled in."

"What?" Bella shook her head. "You don't

even know what you're talking about, Kitty! My mum was the one who found the cottage. And I never wanted to come on holiday with someone like you!"

Frankie was looking between them anxiously. He'd dropped the ball now, and he was turning his head from Bella to Kitty as they argued. His tail drooped between his legs, and he whimpered.

"See! You're upsetting him!" Bella cried. "It's OK, Frankie." She crouched down to stroke him.

"Don't you dare touch him!" Kitty yelled, and she tried to grab Frankie, to pick him up and take him away from Bella. But Frankie shot away from her nervously, and she twisted to catch him, overbalanced, and half fell against Bella, accidentally pushing her over.

Bella yelped as she fell with her weight on her hurt ankle, and Kitty sprang back, shocked. She hadn't meant to hurt Bella at all, and that sudden cry had made her see what she was doing.

"Sorry," she said quietly, holding out her hand to pull Bella back up. Frankie was weaving between them, whining and frightened and showing his teeth.

"Leave me alone," Bella snapped. "I hate you, Kitty. You pretend to be so nice, and you're just a bully."

"What do you mean?" Kitty whispered, going white.

"All that stuff you were doing at school last week – even stealing my medals, and don't even think about pretending you didn't."

"You don't understand. . ." Kitty began.

"Yes, I do!" Bella got up and hurried limping around the side of the house to the back garden. "You were meant to be my friend!" she called.

"No!" Kitty's voice rose in a wail. "It isn't like that." Except it was exactly like that, she realized guiltily.

Frankie barked sharply, and then growled at Kitty. She stared at him in horror – he'd never made a noise like that. Not even when she'd accidentally trod on his tail. "It's OK, Frankie," she tried to say, but her voice wobbled and came out all high and funny, and he backed away from her. Then he dashed out of the gate and over the road to the riverbank.

8

Kitty ran after him, calling frantically. Bella was right – she was so horrible. She'd been hurt by Louisa abandoning her, but she should never have taken it out on Bella. Panting and slipping over the stones, she ran up and down the bank, but she couldn't see Frankie anywhere.

She had to stop after a while, just to catch her breath – she sat on a rock and leaned her elbows on her knees, gasping. The water splashed and glittered over the stones, and Kitty wondered anxiously if Frankie would go in. He'd stood watching the water with her and Dad before, and he'd tried drinking it, but he hadn't been sure about it. If he was really upset though, and he wanted to get as far away from Kitty and Bella shouting as he could? Would he? The river wasn't very deep here; it was hardly more than a covering over the pebbles, but it ran very fast, and it got narrower and deeper not far downstream. Definitely deep and fast enough to carry away a puppy who wasn't used to water.

"Please, no..." Kitty whispered to herself. She got up, still breathing fast, but she could shout again. "Here, Frankie! Frankie, come on!" She was trying so hard to sound calm, but she could hear the note of panic in her voice. If he heard her, he might even run further away. She swallowed hard and tried to smile, to make herself sound happy. Miss Porter, who ran the school choir, had promised them that worked.

But it felt like the smile was stretching her face the wrong way. "Frankie, where are you?"

There was a rattling noise of stones, and she whirled round, hoping to see a feathery little golden dog creeping towards her. But it was Bella.

"I heard you calling! Is he lost?" Bella demanded.

Kitty didn't even think of a sharp answer. She just nodded. "I scared him away by shouting. He ran down here but I can't see him anywhere. Do you think he might have gone in the river?"

Bella frowned worriedly. "I don't think so... He never looked that keen on getting wet, not like Shadow." She swallowed. "I'm sorry, Kitty, it was me that left the gate open."

Kitty sighed. "Only because I was shouting at

you." She stared at the water so she didn't have to look at Bella. "I'm the one who should be sorry. About everything."

She could feel Bella tensing up beside her. "Let's just find him. Which way did he go, could you tell?"

"I think it was this way." Kitty pointed upstream. "But I went up there for ages, calling him. I went as far as the bridge. But I suppose if he was still scared he might not have come out." She swallowed, hating the idea that Frankie was scared of her. Dogs remembered things like that. Shadow knew exactly where the vet was – he ducked down and hid if they even drove past in the car. When they actually had to go to the vet, he behaved like an angel, always, and even gave the vet his paw to shake, but it was obvious that he hated being there. What if Frankie always thought of her as a scary, angry, shouting person from now on? What if he never wanted to come back?

"Please let us find him," Kitty kept whispering to herself as the two of them walked along the riverbank, searching and calling. "Is your ankle all right?"

"It'll be OK. Maybe we should go back and get the dog treats?" Bella suggested. "He'd come if he heard us rattling the bag, wouldn't he?"

"I suppose so." Kitty nodded, but she didn't turn back for the house. "It's just ... I don't want to go back – what if we miss him?" Her voice shook, and she felt tears running down her nose. "Or he thinks we're not bothering to look for him?"

"He wouldn't think that," Bella said, but she

looked worried. "All right. We'll stay here."
She sighed, and grabbed Kitty's hand. "We will
find him. It'll be OK. Frankie! Come on, here,
Frankie."

Kitty sniffed and joined in. A tiny bit of
her was surprised and delighted that Bella
was being so nice, at what a good friend she
was, but mostly she was still worried about
Frankie. They walked up the bank of the river,
calling, peering under bushes – and every so
often looking worriedly out over the water.
"He wouldn't. . ." Kitty whispered, and Bella
squeezed her hand.

"Listen!" Kitty hissed suddenly. They were
coming up to the bridge again, and she could
hear a scuffling noise, somewhere underneath, it
sounded like. "Frankie?" she called hopefully. "Is

that you? Where are you?" They'd been calling him for so long that she expected a squirrel to dart out instead, or maybe another dog out on a walk. But a small golden-haired dachshund dashed across the pebbles towards them, barking excitedly.

"Frankie!" Kitty knelt down, reaching out to hug him, not even noticing that the pebbles were on the waterline and her leggings were getting soaked. He came bouncing towards her, ears flapping, and she held out her arms. She had a moment of panic – what if he wouldn't let her? What if he thought she was too loud and frightening? But he leapt at her, licking her face all over and letting out little squeaks and whines of excitement.

"Where did you go? We were looking for you – we were so worried about you!" Kitty

gasped. "Oh, you're such a good boy, you came back." She stood up, cuddling him, and stood close to Bella to let her stroke him too. She felt Frankie twitch, as if he remembered the argument, but he let Bella stroke him, and they fussed over him together.

"We should go back," Kitty said, looking at

Bella worriedly. "Isn't your ankle hurting?"

Bella made a face. "Yes. Lots – I wasn't noticing it while I was worried about Frankie."

She was quite pale, Kitty noticed, frowning. As though it really was hurting. "I need to hold on to Frankie, just in case; I haven't got his lead and I wouldn't trust him not to run off again. . . But I can tuck him under my arm, and you can lean on my other side." Then she grinned. "No, I know. I'll do what Dad did. Frankie, come on, look." She held out the big kangaroo pocket on the front of her sweatshirt dress. "You can fit in here. I bet you're tired, after all that running. You liked Dad's pocket, didn't you, and this one's nicer." She wriggled him in, and Bella started to laugh.

"He sticks out both ends!"

Kitty looked down – it was true, Frankie's

head and front paws stuck out on one side of her pocket, and his tail at the other.

"I hope Mum's not looking out of the window when we get back. She got me this dress new for going on holiday. But now I can hold you up and you can half walk, half hop." She wrapped her arm round Bella's waist, and Bella put one arm around her shoulders. Frankie peered out curiously to see what they were doing.

"Ooooh, ow," Bella muttered. "No, it's OK. You're helping. I think it just got worse while we were standing still, that's all."

"I can't believe we're doing this," Kitty said suddenly, a few steps later. "That you're actually talking to me. After – everything."

"Me neither," Bella muttered. "I swore I was never ever going to talk to you again.

But Mum and Dad sort of ruined that plan."

Kitty swallowed. "I know I keep saying I'm sorry. But I am. I was so horrible. It was just – Louisa stopped talking to me, and we've been friends since school started, and I couldn't understand..."

"So you picked on me to make yourself look popular," Bella snapped back.

"Yes." Kitty stared down at her feet, ashamed.

"I can see the cottage." Bella sighed with relief. "I'm going to sit on that swing thing."

Kitty pulled Bella's arm around her neck tighter, and they limped the last few steps to the gate and across the garden, so Bella could collapse on the swing. "Oh! I was going to put Frankie on you, but he's asleep." She slid her hand underneath the little dog's silky tummy and drew him out of her pocket, floppy with sleep. "Put him on your knee."

Frankie half opened one eye, and then slumped down on Bella. He started to make little whistly snores, and Bella giggled and patted the seat next to her, telling Kitty to sit down too.

They sat next to each other, Kitty gently rocking the swing with her foot, not talking. It was nice. Kitty wondered if she ought to try and explain some more to Bella, but Bella didn't seem to want her to. She glanced sideways at her, but Bella was just smiling down at Frankie.

Frankie suddenly snorted, and rolled over on Bella's lap, lying there with his paws in the air, and pink skin showing through the gold of his fur. In the distance, Kitty thought she could hear the others coming back – she could hear the boys giggling over something.

"We could take Frankie for a walk tomorrow," she suggested shyly. "If you think your ankle might be better."

Bella half smiled at her, and then nodded. "Maybe it will be."

"I really am sorry," Kitty whispered. "Do you think we can ever be friends again properly?"

Bella sighed, and wriggled herself a little closer to Kitty. Then she slipped her hand under Frankie's shoulders, and moved him so he was half on Kitty's knee too. They were sharing him.

"Thank you." Kitty rubbed her hand over Frankie's smooth domed head, and he opened one eye, staring up at them lazily for a moment. Then he turned over and snuggled himself back to sleep, curled up across both their laps.

Look out for more by
HOLLY WEBB

A Cat Called PENGUIN

HOLLY WEBB

Illustrated by Polly Dunbar

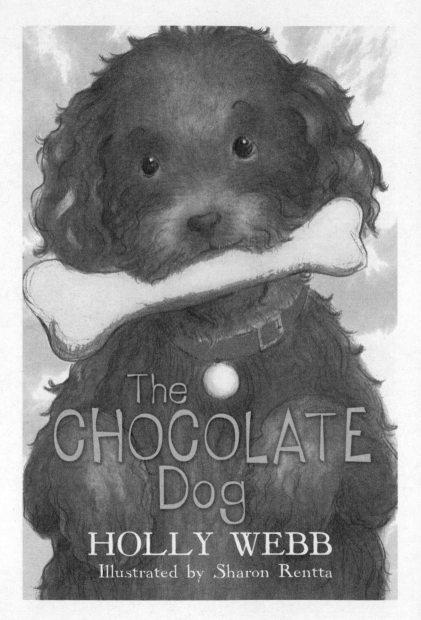

The
CHOCOLATE
Dog

HOLLY WEBB

Illustrated by Sharon Rentta

LOOKING for Bear

HOLLY WEBB

Illustrated by Helen Stephens

A TiGER Tale

HOLLY WEBB

Illustrated by Catherine Rayner

HOLLY WEBB

Illustrated by Hannah Whitty

The Truffle Mouse

Turn over for a sneak peek of

HOLLY WEBB

Illustrated by Sharon Rentta

The
Midnight
Panda

3

James looked cautiously around his bedroom. He'd avoided coming upstairs since he came back from school. He'd done his homework at the kitchen table, saying it was tricky and he needed help, and then pleaded with Mum for some PlayStation time after dinner. But he couldn't put bedtime off any longer.

It was still quite light, the evening sun golden and warm. But James felt shivery. It was the way he had to keep turning round, to check there wasn't anything behind him.

Would the bear come back? James had a horrible sense that he wasn't alone. That something was waiting for him. The shadows around the wardrobe looked darker than they ought to be, thick and treacle-sticky. He had left the door open, and the space out on the landing was warmer and softer and more welcoming than the shadows of his room. James longed to go back out there – but how could he explain to Mum and Dad that he wanted to sleep on the landing instead of in his own bedroom? They knew he was scared of the dark, but James was sure that they didn't know what it really felt like. Mum had promised him that he'd grow out of it, and not to worry. But how was he supposed to stop himself worrying? He couldn't just turn worrying off.

James put his pyjamas on, occasionally whirling round to check that he wasn't being crept up on. Then he stood looking at his bed. He wasn't getting in it. He hadn't quite got as far as saying that to himself until now, but he was sure. He couldn't. What if he had to lie there for hours like he had last night? Watching the bear as the bear watched him? It had felt like hours, anyway.

The light was fading now. James could almost see the shadows, creeping further out from under his bed and behind the wardrobe. He picked up the fleecy blanket from the end of his bed and wrapped it round his shoulders like a cloak, sinking his chin down underneath the folds, so the dark couldn't get at him. He stared fixedly at the wardrobe, but there was no bear. Not yet.

Something rustled outside his window, and

James jumped round, his heart hammering. Just a bird. Or perhaps next door's cat. James turned away, shivering a little, and then gasped as a huge, shadowy thing loomed out for a second between his wardrobe and the door. The bear!

It was gone almost as quickly as it had appeared, but James knew it would be back – and that he couldn't stand being in his room, waiting.

He wouldn't do it! He didn't have to... Mum and Dad thought he was in bed, so that was OK. He would just sleep somewhere else. Somewhere really safe, away from bears.

James's feet had decided where he was going before he even thought of it. He was already hurrying along the landing and into Anna's room when he understood. Anna was the bravest person he knew. She wasn't scared of big dogs (it was a favourite family story that she had disappeared during a barbecue at Uncle Jake's house and been found trying to ride his huge Dobermann like a pony). She actually quite liked spiders. She always volunteered to be the one to rescue them with a jam jar and a bit of cardboard, and she talked to them lovingly as she took them outside to the garden, telling them how much nicer it was outside, and how sorry she was if the spider had been upset by Mum screaming, and that she would never, ever let Mum suck them up with the vacuum cleaner, like she threatened she would.

The only thing Anna was scared of was eggs – she said they were weird and wobbly and she wasn't eating anything that came out of a chicken's bum anyway. But she made an exception for cake – if she couldn't see the egg, she didn't mind pretending it wasn't there.

James would sleep in Anna's room, and she could protect him from the bear. She would probably thump it over the head with a book and tell it to get lost. James trotted into her room, feeling hugely relieved. Anna would understand about the bear – he should have told her about it as soon as they got home from school. In fact, she'd probably have been able to get rid of it straight away. She'd probably tease him a bit – but she did that all the time anyway. James wouldn't mind if she laughed at him, as long as she chased away the bear. He was just starting to tell Anna that he'd been stupid, and he needed her help, when he realized she wasn't actually there.

She was at swimming club. James sat down on her bed with a huff. He'd forgotten. Anna wouldn't be back for ages. And he was so tired. He couldn't stay up until she got back and explain it all then, he just couldn't. He looked enviously at Anna's warm, comfortable bed, beautifully free of bears, and thought about just getting in it. Except if Anna walked in and found him in her bed, she'd make a great fuss, and Mum would send him back to his own room. And Anna would be coming home just when it was getting dark, and ghost bears were properly coming out. No. He couldn't let her. It wouldn't be enough even to write a note, James thought, looking around the room anxiously. There was nothing to say that Anna would read it before she turfed him out of her bed. It was too risky.

Anna's bed was a cabin bed, with a desk that stuck out of the side of it, and storage boxes and bags of old clothes and her sleeping bag and all sorts of other stuff underneath. There were even some floor cushions, from when Anna decided to make it into a den. James sighed with happiness and crawled into the dim little space, laying out the cushions and pulling Anna's sleeping bag over himself. It was perfect. He would be quite safe from bears overnight with Anna there. If a bear turned up, Anna would chase it away, and if it didn't, he'd just explain to Anna in the morning why he was under her bed.

He huddled the sleeping bag up around his

ears, and it was as if sleep came with it, wrapping him in a soft cocoon of warmth. James didn't wake at all when Anna banged open the door and flung down her swimming bag and clattered around the room getting ready for bed. He slept on, warm and safe and certain that no ghost bear would dare raise a paw against his sister.

HOLLY has always loved animals.
As a child she had two dogs, a
cat, and at one point, nine gerbils
(an accident). Holly's other love is
books. Holly now lives in Reading
with her husband, three sons
and three very spoilt cats.